## LACHESIS' ALLOTMENT

A Short Collection of Notes, Observations,
Questions, and Thoughts

# Lachesis' allotment

*a short collection
of notes,
observations, questions,
and thoughts*

diana r.a. morris

ISBN 978-1-7320022-1-0 (Trade Paperback)
ISBN 978-1-7320022-0-3 (E-Book)

Library of Congress Control Number 2018901734

www.dianaramorris.com

*For my family—the one I was born into, and the one I've made along the way.*

# Contents

## CHAPTER 0: The Introduction

IN GREEK MYTHOLOGY, THE PHYSICAL manifestations of life and destiny were three sisters known as the Moirai, or Fates, and they were not to be trifled with. Whereas Clotho, the eldest sister, was in charge of spinning the thread of life and Atropos, the youngest, was in charge of cutting it, it was the middle sister, Lachesis (pronounced *lack-eh-sis*), who had all the fun—she decided exactly how much thread each person was allotted and what they did with their piece.

While I don't necessarily believe that there is one specific, predetermined path for each person, I do know that the thread woven throughout my life has stitched together a very interesting tapestry. As my story weaves in and out of other people's lives, some areas have snagged and others have formed a beautiful design, but either way, I wouldn't trade this fabric for any other. So Lachesis, if you're reading this, thanks for hooking me up.

## CHAPTER 1: Note to Self
### (and Those Following Along at Home)

SCREW DOUBT AND GO FOR IT. The worst that can happen is "no." The best that can happen remains to be seen.

# TRANSIENT BONDS

SCREENPLAY BY
DIANA R.A. MORRIS

INT. OLIVIA CLARKSON'S HOME — DAY

Inside of a small, tasteful studio apartment in Jamaica Plain, MA, a futon is pushed against the wall, and dishes are drying on the kitchen countertop. The curtains are pulled back, and the late morning sun casts a warm glow on an unrolled yoga mat and an overflowing bookshelf.

OLIVIA CLARKSON is a twentysomething-year-old woman studying her reflection in a full-length mirror. She has a clothes hanger in each hand—the first holding a dress and the second holding a blouse. Olivia switches between the two, her brow furrowed and her head tilting from side to side. She groans softly.

                    OLIVIA
          (muttering under her breath)
       This is stupid.

She throws the two pieces to the floor and walks to the clothing rack to her left, angrily shoving fabric from one side to the other. She grimaces as she selects another dress.

                    OLIVIA
          Why do I care so much? It's just
          coffee.

                                        CUT TO:

INT. BETHANY AND FREDERICK LEWIS' HOME — DAY

BETHANY and FREDERICK LEWIS, both in their late
twenties, are in their two-story brownstone in
the Beacon Hill neighborhood of Boston, MA.
With its open floor plan and contemporary decor,
the unit has the air of an art gallery housed in
a luxury hotel. Framed paintings and photographs
cover the walls, and tasteful sculptures are
displayed throughout the rooms. The space is
designed for public consumption, and only a few
personal items are visible to the naked eye.

Bethany and Frederick are seated at the kitchen
island. Frederick is reading the newspaper,
and Bethany is typing on her laptop. Both are
silent. At the sound of a timer, Bethany rises
from her seat and walks over to an espresso
maker sitting on a marble countertop.

Bethany calls over her shoulder as she takes a
mug out of the cabinet.

                    BETHANY
          Are you sure you don't want one?

Frederick's eyes are focused on an article in the
business section of the paper, and he addresses
Bethany without looking up.

                    FREDERICK
          I'm sure.

He looks up from the paper and watches Bethany
move from one cabinet to another.

                    FREDERICK
          Aren't you going out for coffee in
          about an hour?

Bethany shrugs as she pours the steaming espresso
and uses a small, stainless-steel milk pitcher to
carefully draw a four-leaf clover into the cream.

                    BETHANY
          That's the plan.

Bethany remains focused on her design.

Frederick folds the paper and places it in front
of him.

FREDERICK
So...are you going to cancel?

Bethany looks up from the mug and places the
pitcher on the counter.

BETHANY
Why would I cancel?

Frederick studies Bethany's face to gauge her
reaction before responding.

FREDERICK
Because you hardly talk about this
meeting, and when you do talk about
it, you're brainstorming ways to
bail.

Bethany picks up the mug and walks back to her
seat, lowering herself slowly. She takes a small
sip of the steaming drink before responding.

BETHANY
You make me sound horrible.

Frederick smiles and rubs Bethany's leg.

                    FREDERICK
          No, I don't. I make you sound
          nervous. Unsure. Skeptical.

Bethany stares at the foam in the mug, lost in
thought.

## CHAPTER 2: No [Person] Is an Island

BY DESIGN, HUMAN BEINGS ARE social creatures.[1] We need companionship in order to survive and thrive in the world. Even the staunchest member of the "I hate people" club yearns for authentic, nourishing connections with other people. This need for connection makes itself known from

---

1 This fact has been reviewed repeatedly. See, for example, Debra Umberson and Jennifer Karas Montez's (2011) review of how social ties impact our behavioral, psychosocial, and physiological development in "Social Relationships and Health: A Flashpoint for Health Policy," Supplement, Journal of Health and Social Behavior 51 (2010): S54–S66, https://www.ncbi.nlm.nih.gov/pmc/articles/PMC3150158, or listen to the lyrics of Andrew Gold's "Thank You for Being a Friend," which served as the soundtrack for Dorothy, Blanche, Rose, and Sophia's shenanigans on *The Golden Girls*.

the minute we enter the world. Biologically, we need others to help us when we are unable to feed, clothe, and protect ourselves, and as we get older, this support transitions into helping us define who we are and what values we hold dear.[2]

Even before we begin to discover sexuality and navigate the needs associated with it, we surround ourselves with people who meet our nonsexual social and emotional desires, and as we continue through life, these unions grow. Because of this, I wholeheartedly believe that, though love stories tend to focus on the work of Cupid, falling in platonic love is every bit as magical as falling in romantic love, and, for me, its wonder is only overshadowed by that of the transformation from lovers or friends to strangers.

Do you remember your first friend? I do. Her name was Martha,[3] and sometimes I turn to Google in an attempt to find her and reconnect. Based on my sleuthing, I think she still lives somewhere around where we grew up, but she doesn't appear to have any social media accounts, so for now she is a connection that will remain enshrined in my past.

Back in the day, Martha and I were inseparable. Some of my most vivid childhood memories are of visits to her house, where we would play soccer and watch *Spice World*. Those

---

2 It should be noted that, while the emphasis on communal connections versus independent progression is influenced by culture and environment, the core tenets of interdependence remain constant among all humans.

3 No, it wasn't, but in the interest of protecting her privacy, I've given her this name instead. Who knows, maybe she'll read this and recognize herself. If so, hey girl! I hope all is well.

were, for all intents and purposes, wonderful times, but I remember becoming disillusioned with our friendship one day and attempting to frame her.

I kid you not, I tried to frame her.

"How?" you may ask. Well, I wrote a note calling myself all sorts of names[4] and then "found" it crumpled up on the floor in our classroom. Upon my "discovery," I brought the note to my teacher and played the part of a distraught, innocent target. I'm sure I had some specific end goal for this in mind, but it escapes me now. What I do remember is my mother being called in for a meeting with my teacher to discuss what had happened.[5] Although my teacher believed my story without hesitation, my mom took one look at the note and calmly asked me why I wrote it. Apparently she had some magical mother's intuition that made her recognize the paper from a notebook she had bought me earlier that year.[6] Needless to say, my plan didn't work, but in true childlike fashion, whatever had been bothering me was quickly forgotten, and Martha and I returned to playing soccer and watching Oscar-contending films.

While I no longer go around committing minor crimes against my friends when I feel neglected or threatened, I do take friendships very seriously. Maturity, time, and experience

---

4 I essentially made my own version of a Burn Book. Regina George (from the cinematic classic *Mean Girls*) would have been so proud.

5 In true nerd fashion, I went to the same school my mother taught at.

6 Or maybe she just recognized my handwriting; it's hard to tell. Either way, she just laughs whenever I bring it up now. So smug.

have taught me that there are levels to the relationships I cultivate, and not everyone is able to meet the requirements I have. I've also become keenly aware that the different ways people operationalize social entanglements are hardly ever right or wrong—they just are what they are.

For a long time, I took things to heart and Monday-morning-quarterbacked each changing tide in my relationships with other people. As I replayed the mental footage of my connections, I positioned myself as both player and spectator, and placed all responsibility for what happened on my shoulders. When a relationship wasn't going as well as I wanted or if it wasn't meeting the potential I saw in it, a litany of questions would unfurl: Was it something I said? Something I didn't say? If I had done $x$, would the other person have done $y$? What could I do to fix what was wrong?

Before we continue, I want to take this time to make an important distinction: While I am a big advocate of honest reflection and self-improvement, this is not what I was doing. Over time, the type of evaluation and self-critiquing to which I subscribed became exhausting and counterproductive. It chipped away at my sense of self and took away from the amazing relationships I did have—ones that I didn't have to tear myself down and break myself into pieces to maintain.

The people who I spent so much mental and emotional energy on never met the expectations I had for them, and they never accepted what I so desperately wanted to give. In hindsight, I realize that what is meant for me will never leave me, and everything has a season—some just last longer than others.

One of the most interesting topics of conversation that repeatedly comes up with associates and friends has been the connections that remain and those that have dissolved, either expectedly or by surprise.

Central to the formation of any relationship, whether it be platonic or romantic, is a constant exchange of energy that provides sustenance and growth for those involved. Conversely, at the very core of the dissolution of any relationship is an imbalance of this energy exchange, usually in the form of an absence, such as of care, contact, or expressed interest. This, as I mentioned earlier, doesn't get nearly the level of shine I think it deserves.

How is it that we can have firsthand experience of something and watch it dwindle down to nothing? And I'm not talking about toxic partnerships that cause harm, or associations that have not had time to broker any real investment. I'm talking about relationships that have burrowed themselves into the very core of our existence and have played a pivotal role in how we view and experience the world. It takes time and energy to build something of that magnitude, and the building process, while tedious, often yields a great return on investment. Doesn't that make it worth it?

Assuming that it does, to then see that beautiful structure in all its glory, to envision what it can look like as time goes on, and to wander its halls and run your hands along its grooves, how can the aforementioned imbalance enter the picture? How can people watch everything crumble and decide to let absence grow like ivy on an abandoned building?

For me, this is where the fear sets in, the element that I don't quite know how to navigate. Rationally, I know it all boils down to redefining success and failure and extending grace to all the factors you can't control, but still. Even with this objective understanding, doesn't a part of you always wonder what happened? Was there something that you should have seen coming, some hint by way of a crack in the foundation or a creaking, wobbly step that groaned every time you climbed?

At what point do people become aware of the disintegration? At what point do they no longer care? At what point do we decide to cut the thread that unites us with another?

What was it for you? Do you remember your first real breakup, friend or otherwise? When did you realize that that partnership was no longer worth the energy you put into it? Was your pulling away the first step toward the end, or were you simply following the trail that someone else blazed before you?

Me? I'm still figuring that out. I'm still determining what it means to let go without feeling as though I've given up. Because truly, after I do all the mental and emotional work to give someone access to my blueprints and they've gotten to know me and see what I can offer, for them to then decide that it's not what they want after all . . . I used to take this as a direct reflection of me and who I am. Now I see it as a signal of where to look next.

It all goes back to redefining success and failure and having faith in the unknown. It's about trusting that even if the building I create doesn't end up being a permanent structure, there are plenty of buildings ready for me to design with the right person(s).

I don't know if Martha ever found out about the note, but I do know our friendship lasted as long as childhood friendships could before life took over and we drifted apart. I also know that in the years since, I've fallen in and out of love with people who have entered my life and stayed and others who have entered and exited. And now, when I take a step back and look at the tapestry of my life so far, I'm grateful for each and every piece of stitching left behind.

INT. TRIDENT BOOKSELLERS & CAFÉ — DAY

Bethany walks through the front door of the
small bookstore on Newbury Street that doubles
as a café. It is a slow day, and both the
bookstore and the dining area are relatively
empty. She scans the space and sees A HOSTESS at
the front and A WAITER serving other PATRONS.
Olivia is squatting down in one of the aisles, a
book balanced on each knee and one in her hand.
Bethany slowly walks over to her.

                    BETHANY
          Olivia?

Olivia looks up, startled. Her face is
expressionless for a moment before a smile
spreads across her lips. The smile does not
quite meet her eyes.

                    OLIVIA
          Oh wow. Bethany. Hi.

Olivia quickly puts the books back on the shelf
and stands to face Bethany.

                    OLIVIA
          It's so nice to see you.

Olivia and Bethany fall into a beat of silence
before both begin to speak.

          OLIVIA                    BETHANY
Should we go grab a seat?  Do you want to get
                            a table?

Olivia and Bethany smile genuinely at each other
and, without another word, walk over to the
hostess.

                 THE HOSTESS
          How many of you will be joining us
          today?

                    BETHANY
          Just two, thank you.

The hostess takes two menus from the stack and
moves from behind the podium.

                    THE HOSTESS
          If you'll follow me this way.


Bethany and Olivia sit. The hostess smiles.

                    THE HOSTESS
          Your server will be right with you.


Olivia and Bethany are silent as the hostess
walks away. The two women look around the dining
area, their eyes focusing on everything except
each other. Their attention is brought back to
the table when the waiter arrives.

                    THE WAITER
               Can I get you ladies started with
               anything to drink?

                    BETHANY
          I'd like a coffee, please. Black.


The waiter turns to Olivia.

                    THE WAITER
               And for you?

                    OLIVIA
          Water is fine, thank you.

                    THE WAITER
          Do you need more time to look at the
          menu, or are you ready to order?

                     OLIVIA
          Oh, we're not eating. Just the
          drinks, thank you.

Bethany looks at Olivia for a moment before
turning her attention to the waiter. She smiles.

                    BETHANY
          What she said.

The waiter nods and collects their menus.

                    THE WAITER
          I'll have those right out to you.

The waiter walks away, and Olivia and Bethany
fall back into silence. It lasts until the
waiter returns a few moments later with their
drinks.

                     OLIVIA
          What cup is that today?

Bethany looks up from scanning the condiment
tray for sugar, confusion etching her features.

                    BETHANY

          Excuse me?

Olivia points to the coffee in front of her.

                    OLIVIA

          How many cups of coffee have you had
          so far?

                    BETHANY
              (smiling sheepishly)
          This is only my second. I've cut back.

Olivia smiles and gently sips her water. The two
women fall back into silence. This time it is
Bethany who breaks it.

                    BETHANY

          Okay. Why is this so weird?

Olivia looks at her but says nothing.

                    BETHANY

          It's not just me, right? Something
          feels off.

Olivia continues to look at Bethany, her eyes
squinting slightly as she tilts her head to the
left.

                    OLIVIA
          What would "on" look like to you?

Bethany opens her mouth to respond but seems to
think better of it. Olivia continues.

                    OLIVIA
          I mean, we haven't spoken since
          graduation, and to be honest, I'm not
          quite sure why you contacted me.

Bethany tries unsuccessfully to hide the hurt
that flashes across her face. She takes a sip of
coffee before responding.

                    BETHANY
          Why did you say yes?

Olivia is silent.

                    BETHANY
          Exactly. Because deep down you want
          to know how my life is going, just as
          I want to know about yours.

A tense silence swoops down and lingers before
the waiter walks over with a coffee pot and
pitcher of water.

                    THE WAITER
          (clearing his throat gently as he
          tops off their beverages)
       Can I get you two anything else?

The women say nothing, their eyes trained on
each other.

                    THE WAITER
       Okay, well, let me know if you need
       anything.

He quickly turns and walks away.

                    OLIVIA
          (watching Bethany absentmindedly
          stir her coffee)
       I said yes because I had nothing
       better to do today and figured that
       there are worst ways to spend a
       Saturday afternoon.

Bethany slowly raises the cup to her lips and
takes a sip.

                    BETHANY
       And how has it been going for you so
       far?

                         OLIVIA
                  (smiling sarcastically)
            Oh, just swimmingly.

She picks up her own glass and sips.

                         OLIVIA
            How about you? Why did you ask?

                         BETHANY
            I saw no reason not to. We're both in
            Boston now, so...

Olivia puts down her glass.

                         OLIVIA
                  (smoothing out the napkin in front
                  of her)
            I moved back nine months ago.

Bethany waits until Olivia looks at her before
responding.

                         BETHANY
            Better late than never, right?

Olivia doesn't respond.

Bethany slowly takes another sip of her coffee
before putting the cup down. She runs her finger
around the rim.

                    BETHANY
          Frederick says hi, by the way.

Olivia looks at her, surprised.

                    OLIVIA
          Oh wow, you keep in contact? How
          is he? I haven't spoken to him in
          forever.

                    BETHANY
          He's doing well. We're actually...

She clears her throat.

                    BETHANY
          He and I...

She moves her left hand onto the table. Up until
this moment, it had been resting on her lap.

                    BETHANY
          We're married.

Olivia looks from Bethany's face to her hand,
her eyes resting on the stacked silver bands
for several seconds. She picks up her water and
takes a deep swallow.

                    OLIVIA
          Congratulations.

She puts down her glass.

                    OLIVIA
          When did that happen?

Bethany watches Olivia, trying to get a sense of
what she is thinking.

                    BETHANY
          Next week makes three years.

                    OLIVIA
          Oh wow.

                    BETHANY
          Olivia...

Olivia holds up a hand, signaling for her to stop.

                    OLIVIA
          Can we not?

Olivia purses her lips together and takes a deep
breath, letting it out slowly.

                    OLIVIA
          So what else is new?

Bethany thinks for a moment.

                    BETHANY
          Nothing much really. I'm still
          working at the firm.

Olivia looks at her with questions in her eyes.

                    OLIVIA
          What firm?

Bethany squints slightly, surprised by the
question.

                    BETHANY
          The law firm. I went to law school
          after graduation and then started
          working downtown. I thought I told
          you.

A small smile passes over Olivia's lips. It's
both reflective and sad.

                    OLIVIA
          We haven't spoken-

                    BETHANY
          -since graduation, yeah, I know,
          but...I had things up online, so I
          thought...

Olivia takes another sip of her water and
signals for the waiter.

                    THE WAITER
          How are you ladies doing over here?

                     OLIVIA
          Can we have the check, please?

Bethany looks at Olivia.

Olivia keeps her gaze on the waiter.

                    THE WAITER
          Of course.

He looks from one woman to the other.

                    THE WAITER
          Would you like me to put in an order
          for anything to take on your way out?

                     BETHANY
              (her gaze is still trained on
              Olivia)
          No, I think we're done.

                    THE WAITER
          Okay, I'll have your check right
          out to you.

He leaves the table, and Olivia looks at Bethany.

                    OLIVIA
          This was a great suggestion. Thanks
          for the invite.

                    BETHANY
          Is that sarcasm?

                    OLIVIA
          Yes, it is.


Bethany shakes her head and opens her mouth to
respond. Before she can get a word out, the
waiter returns with the check.

                  THE WAITER
          Here you go, whenever you're ready.


He turns to leave, but Olivia stops him.

                    OLIVIA
          We're ready now.


Bethany reaches into her purse, pulls out her
wallet, and hands the waiter a credit card. The
waiter takes the payment for processing, and
once he leaves, Bethany begins.

                    BETHANY
          Why are you so mad at me?

Olivia jerks back slightly as if she's been slapped.

                    OLIVIA
          I'm not mad, I'm—

                    BETHANY
          —Bullshit. You've been acting like
          I forced you here against your will
          or something, as though I've done
          something wrong.

                    OLIVIA
               (continuing on as if Bethany
               hadn't spoken)
          —indifferent.

Bethany looks at her silently.

                    THE WAITER
               (walking over with a smile and
               Bethany's receipt and card)
          Thank you both for coming in. Enjoy
          the rest of your day.

He turns and leaves. Bethany doesn't move. Olivia looks at her.

                    OLIVIA
          Are you going to take your card,
          or...?

Bethany looks at Olivia for another second before signing the receipt and placing the card back in her wallet.

Olivia stands first, slipping her arms into her peacoat. Bethany rises and does the same. Once their coats are on, Olivia and Bethany walk out of the bookstore and into the brisk afternoon.

EXT. OUTSIDE OF TRIDENT BOOKSELLERS & CAFÉ — DAY

                    OLIVIA
          Well, it was good seeing you.

Bethany raises an eyebrow.

                    OLIVIA
          No, seriously, it was. I'm happy
          things are going well for you. Tell
          Frederick I say hi.

                    BETHANY
          So, that's it?

Olivia looks at the woman in front of her.

                    OLIVIA
          Is what it?

                    BETHANY
          You haven't told me anything about
          yourself or what you've been up to
          these last few years.

Olivia takes a deep, exasperated breath and
stuffs her hands in her pockets.

                    OLIVIA
          Well, let's see...

She tilts her head as if thinking.

                    OLIVIA
          After graduation I traveled a bit
          before settling in Portland. I started
          an MBA program, I hated the MBA
          program, so I left the MBA program,
          and now I'm back here working with a
          start-up downtown and...yeah.

She shrugs.

                    OLIVIA
          That's basically it.

                    BETHANY
               (nodding knowingly)
          Computers in management.

Olivia raises an eyebrow, confused.

                    OLIVIA
          Huh?

                    BETHANY
               (with emphasis and a small wave of
               her hands, as if repeating herself
               will jog Olivia's memory)
          Computers in management...

Olivia continues to look at her, confused.

                    BETHANY
          You know, that class we had to take
          freshman year. We all hated it, but
          you understood it so much better than
          anyone else.

                    OLIVIA
          Oh.

She shrugs.

                    OLIVIA
          Yeah, well the thought of looking at
          Excel for the rest of my life quickly
          lost its appeal, so...

She lets her voice trail off.

Bethany smiles and checks her watch.

                    BETHANY
          Do you wanna walk around for a
          little, or do you have somewhere you
          need to be?

Olivia doesn't immediately answer and looks down
the street before turning her attention back to
Bethany.

                    OLIVIA
          Um, yeah...that should be fine, I
          guess.

Olivia and Bethany turn and start down the crowded
sidewalk, their silence interrupted only by the
sounds of the city around them.

CHAPTER 3: Oscar-Worthy Performances

EACH ACTION WE TAKE, EACH interaction we have—those are the scenes of our very own movie. Every person we come in contact with, whether for a moment or for a lifetime, makes up our supporting cast. Some people start off playing such an important role in the films of our lives, only to end up on the cutting room floor, and others start off hidden in the background, only to become our most important costars by the time the credits roll.

Whether it be a drama, a comedy, or a postapocalyptic tale, all we can hope is that our movie is an Oscar-worthy one and that we, the most important critic, will give it two thumbs-up when we leave the theater.

How does that happen? By just being. Being yourself, being true to the script and characters as they unfold, and being open to the spoilers and plot twists that come your way. After all, that's life, ya know?

EXT. BOSTON PUBLIC GARDEN — DAY

Bethany and Olivia are walking through the
park and talking, their conversation flowing
freer than it did in the café. There are PEOPLE
running, lounging, and otherwise enjoying the
open space.

                    BETHANY
              (looking around the scene
              in front of them)
          Oh man. I haven't been down here in
          so long.

                    OLIVIA
          To the Gardens? This is one of my
          favorite places to run.

                    BETHANY
          Wait, you run down here?

                    OLIVIA
              (nodding)
          Sometimes, depending on my mood.

                    BETHANY
          Holy shit. How far is this from your
          apartment?

Olivia thinks for a moment and then shrugs.

                    OLIVIA
          A little over five miles each way,
          give or take.

                    BETHANY
     Whoa.

                    OLIVIA
          I'm gonna be doing a 5k in a couple
          of months if you wanna join me.

Bethany looks at Olivia with a raised eyebrow.

                    BETHANY
          That's a joke, right?

Olivia laughs.

                    OLIVIA
          Ah yes, how could I forget? You're
          allergic to physical activity.

                    BETHANY
          I just think the whole concept is
          unnatural. Like, what's the rush?

                    BETHANY (CONT'D)
          Where am I going? Can I get there
          quicker by car or the T?[7]

She shakes her head.

                    BETHANY
          I'll stick to the basics of walking,
          thank you very much.

The two women continue walking in silence before
Olivia stops in the middle of the path. A woman
running with a stroller dodges around her,
narrowly avoiding a collision.

                    OLIVIA
          What happened?

She asks the question softly, almost as if the
words have snuck past the cage of her teeth
before she can stop them.

                    BETHANY
              (stopping as well)
          What happened with wha...?

The question dies on Bethany's tongue as she
looks at Olivia. She knows exactly what is being
asked.

---

**7** The T, or trolley, is an aboveground subway that services Boston and neighboring communities.

                    BETHANY
          To be honest, I don't really know.
          I mean...I guess life happened and
          before I knew it...

She shrugs.

Olivia slowly nods, stuffing her hands in her
pockets.

                    OLIVIA
          I can appreciate that, but it's a bit
          of a cop-out, don't you think?

                    BETHANY
             (shrugging)
          I honestly don't know what to tell
          you. I thought about reaching out a
          bunch of times but knew that this
          would happen and...I guess I didn't
          want to have to deal with it.

                    OLIVIA
          So, why deal with it now?

Bethany looks at the ground before focusing her
gaze past Olivia's shoulder.

                    BETHANY
          I realized that I missed my friend.

                    BETHANY (CONT'D)
          And that hurt way more than having to
          explain why I was in a position to
          miss you in the first place.

Olivia allows the response to hang in the air
for a beat.

                         OLIVIA
          What did Frederick say when you told
          him you were coming to meet me?

                        BETHANY
              (smiling sheepishly)
          He was surprised that I didn't
          cancel.

Olivia laughs, and the two women resume walking.

                        BETHANY
          What do you think happened?

Olivia is silent before responding.

                         OLIVIA
          I think you're right, life happened.
          And the way my life was happening
          didn't need to include you anymore,
          and the way yours was happening
          didn't need to include me.

                         BETHANY
                  (grimacing slightly)
            That's kinda harsh, don't you think?

Olivia shrugs.

                         OLIVIA
            It's not meant to be. I mean, we can
            dress it up any way we want, but at
            the end of the day, isn't that what
            it comes down to? The person I was
            when we were roommates isn't the
            person I am today, and the same goes
            for you, I'm sure.

She puts her hands back in her pocket.

                         OLIVIA
            I don't doubt that the core elements
            are still there—I mean, I know they
            are for me—but all the extra stuff
            that comes with them have changed.
            What I needed from people back then
            isn't what I need from people now,
            and I've found new ways to meet those
            needs.

                         BETHANY
                  (nodding)
            No, I know what you mean. It's just
            weird to hear it phrased like that.

She is silent before continuing.

                    BETHANY
          To be honest, I don't really keep in
          contact with the people I thought I
          would at all...which I'm sure you've
          noticed.

                    OLIVIA
               (scoffing)
          Yeah, I've noticed. In the spirit of
          honesty, if you'd reached out to me a
          year ago, I would have ignored you. I
          wouldn't have been ready to do this.

                    BETHANY
          So what's changed in a year?

Olivia takes a deep breath, shaking her head,
the move almost imperceptible.

                    OLIVIA
          I'm learning how to not take things
          like that personally. There was a
          time where I did—especially when it
          came to you. I mean, we went from
          talking every day, to me doing all
          the work, to nothing happening at
          all...it made me question a lot of
          things, but then I was like, fuck it.

                    OLIVIA (CONT'D)
          That shit was too damn exhausting and
          life is too damn short. For the sake
          of my sanity, I'm becoming more aware
          of who I am and what I bring to the
          table, and people are either with it
          or they're not.

Bethany looks at Olivia from the corner of her
eye.

                    BETHANY
          I feel like you were always like
          that, though. That's one of the
          things I remember the most about you.

                    OLIVIA
          Yeah, but it's different from when
          we were in college. Like, deciding
          not to go out on a Thursday when
          everyone is pregaming in the common
          room is very different from sitting
          alone with myself and realizing that
          if I put all my cards on the table
          and someone decides they don't want
          to play anymore, that doesn't mean
          there's anything wrong with the deck
          I have, ya know?

She pauses.

                         OLIVIA
          I'm still figuring out how to frame it
          in my mind, but yeah.

                         BETHANY
               (nodding)
          No, I get it.

The two are silent as they walk a few more paces.

                         BETHANY
          So how did you frame us not talking
          anymore?

                         OLIVIA
          Like we said earlier, it's life.

She lets out a humorless laugh.

                         OLIVIA
          I just didn't realize how wild it
          was until you reached out and then
          again just now when you said you were
          married. Like, in high school, people
          always make plans to visit each other
          in college, but it's kinda expected
          that you'll drift apart as time goes
          on. I guess I was surprised that it
          happened with you. I don't know why I
          expected more from us, but...

She shakes her head.

                    OLIVIA
          I have no idea who you are anymore,
          and you don't know anything about me—
          we only have the memories of who we
          were back in the day. On my end I'm
          trying to line that up with where we
          are today.

Olivia and Bethany walk in silence, each lost in
her own thoughts.

                    BETHANY
          How's your family? Your mom and your
          sister?

                    OLIVIA
          They're good. Maggie's about to start
          her senior year of college.

Bethany stops in her tracks.

                    BETHANY
          Wait...she's a senior? How?

She resumes walking, moving quickly to catch up
to Olivia, who is now several paces in front of
her.

                    BETHANY
          I feel like she was just in
          elementary school.

                    OLIVIA
               (rolling her eyes)
          Tell me about it. I have to keep
          reminding myself that she's not five
          anymore. It's weird and I hate it.

Bethany laughs.

                    OLIVIA
          Mom is good, too. Still teaching
          children well and letting them lead
          the way.

Bethany rolls her eyes and laughs again.

                    OLIVIA
          How about you? How's your family?
          Your mom? Dad?

The laughter slowly dies from Bethany's lips.
She clears her throat.

                    BETHANY
          My mom died a few years ago.

Olivia turns to her sharply, her face a mix of horror and sadness.

                    OLIVIA
          Bethany, I'm so...what happened?

Bethany waves her hand, discomfort radiating from the movement.

                    BETHANY
          It's fine, really. I mean...

She draws in a deep breath and exhales loudly.

                    BETHANY
               She went in for a standard visit,
               and by the time they found the
               tumor...there really wasn't anything
               they could do.

She swallows and clears her throat.

                    BETHANY
               It's actually why...Freddy and I
               were going to have a big wedding and
               make it a whole thing, but things
               happened so fast that...we ended up
               doing things quickly so she could be
               there.

She looks at Olivia with a sad smile.

                    BETHANY
          She and my dad were able to walk me
          down the aisle. Well, for her it was
          more like wheel beside me as I walked,
          but she was there.

She looks away quickly.

                    OLIVIA
          Beth, I had no idea. I'm
          sorry...I...

Her voice breaks as Bethany waves her hand
again, this time with more ease.

                    BETHANY
          Thanks, really, but we're good. I'm
          good. I've had time to work through
          it, so, ya know, here we are.

She looks past Olivia and points to a building
across the street. Olivia follows her gaze.

                    BETHANY
          Look where we are. Do you remember
          how much we used to love this place?

                    OLIVIA
             (swallowing and clearing her
             throat)
          I do. Wanna go in?

                    BETHANY
          Absolutely.

The two women cross the street and approach
their next destination.

## CHAPTER 4: Getting on a First-Name Basis with My Parents

DO YOU KNOW YOUR PARENT or guardian's favorite color? For real—think about it for a second.

It wasn't until I realized I didn't know the answer to this question that it hit me—even though I had lived with my mother and father consistently for thirteen years, and on and off for another fifteen, I didn't really know anything about them.

Sure, I knew how they managed anger and showed love, how their moral compasses were adjusted, and what brought them joy, but even that knowledge was gained and filtered through the lens of childlike wonder.

I didn't really know my mother for the first twenty-odd years of my life, and I never really got the chance to know my father before he passed away.

As I type that out and read it back, it's a saddening thought and a humbling reality.

As I've gotten older, I see a lot of my parents in myself. My father's blood runs through my veins, and his ring adorns my finger, just as his low tolerance for lateness and his love of the written word have shaped my temperament and interests. My mother's height helps me navigate the world with grace, just as her laugh rings out of my mouth as I struggle to tell a joke and her side-eye helps me say so much without uttering a word.

But these things I've picked up from them, where are they from? Who taught them how to cook? How to love? How to exist? Did my mother's seemingly misplaced British accent come from colonialism, as I sometimes joke, or did she live in England at one point?[8] Did my father's tendency to hide emotions come as a result of crying in front of the wrong person at the wrong time?

Who are my parents, and more specifically, who are they outside of that role? How much time do I need to find out the full spectrum of them as people? How much time do I have?

I recently sat down and calculated it. Given her age, the very real health concerns that impact the black community,

---

**8** I did ask, and I was right about the colonialism thing. When she was growing up in Jamaica, nearly all of my mom's teachers were from England.

and the fact that nothing is guaranteed anymore,[9] if I am lucky, I have about twenty more years with my mother. Assuming that I continue my trend of only going home for major holidays and limiting my visits to a maximum of four days and three nights,[10] each calendar year I will hypothetically see her for about eight days a year. When multiplied by the estimated number of years we have left, that's 160 days, which equates to about five to six months of time spent together in person. Again, this is all assuming that I'm lucky.

While she and I have near daily interactions via text, phone calls, and Words with Friends,[11] six months of face-to-face time is nothing in the grand scheme of things. It doesn't even equal the amount of time she carried my heartbeat with hers. Isn't that wild? And now that I know this, what do I do with it?

For starters, I picked up the phone and called. I found out why my mother gave my father a chance all those years ago[12]

---

**9** Between the death of my father during my junior year of college and the twenty-four-hour news cycle, this is as irrefutable as the fact that we inhale oxygen and exhale carbon dioxide.

**10** This time limit is directly related to my patience level when being at home. Among other things, have you tried sleeping on a twin mattress after living with the luxury of a queen? I love that my room is pretty much the same from when I was younger, but come on!

**11** To be honest, I might have to put a stop to this because I'm pretty sure she's cheating, but there's no real way for me to accuse her of this without her reaching through the phone and snatching me up. Although I guess I could show her this chapter?

**12** Turns out, methods of courting haven't changed too much over time, and wingmen, wingwomen, and friends are super important. My dad told one of his friends that he thought my mom was beautiful and that he wanted to get to know her, and that friend told my mom. The rest, as they say, is history.

and how she feels now that he's gone. I found out what she thinks about how her life is unfolding and got a little insight into the woman she was before I entered her world. I'm starting the process of getting to know the woman who raised me as Pauline and not just as "Mommy," and these are some of the most important conversations I think I'll ever have.

And most importantly, most memorably, I found out that her favorite color is purple. And Von's? His was sky blue.

CHAPTER 5 : The Sound of Silence

THE WORST PART OF LOSING SOMEONE is forgetting what they sound like.

I can remember the words—the "Do unto others as you would have them do unto you" that was released as a sermon each time we parted ways and the "Good, better, best. Never let it rest until your good is better and your better best" that served as its partner. But the low bass. The heavy patois. The slow cadence that made every word fall over you like molasses. The delivery of these mantras. Those are the things I miss. Those things have all but faded from my memory.

There was a time when I'd listen to old voicemails just for something to hold onto. "Diana, this is your father calling," as if I didn't have caller ID. As if I wouldn't recognize that voice in a sea of static. However, as with most things in life, those voicemails are long gone, erased the minute I had to get a new phone.

I often wonder what it would be like if he were still here. Would we text? Would he have Facebook? Would he appreciate the wonders of GIFs? That would be a sight to see, but I'm pretty sure I would always dial home just to hear his voice.

I've long since forgotten some of the more mundane conversations and words, but I have a running list of things I wish he could say. At this moment it's the stockpile of bragging rights I've earned him.[13] In a few years it'll be the way he'd introduce himself to his grandchild(ren) at every encounter, regardless of the fact that over time they, too, would be able to pick his voice out of a crowd.

Maybe one day we'll speak again. Until then, I'll keep getting used to the silence.

---

**13** You know what I mean... with parents, your job is their job, your degrees are their degrees, your home is their home. It used to irritate me to no end when I was younger, but now I see that it's a reflection of pride and joy.

CHAPTER 6: Family Matters
(It's So Hard to Say Goodbye)

AS A JUNIOR IN COLLEGE, I had the opportunity to study abroad in Thessaloniki, Greece. It was my first real[14] experience leaving the country, and I prepared a presentation to convince my father to let me live on another continent for an entire semester. The presentation provided a cost-benefit analysis of the experience and had a heavy focus on education, his favorite thing.

14 My first official time abroad was when my family visited Jamaica when I was a baby (which I have no recollection of, but apparently I got lost in the airport looking for my mom), and my second time was during my senior year in high school when I went to the Dominican Republic with some friends. I didn't get lost in the airport that time.

However, the speech was never used because when I started with the question of moving to Greece for a few months, he answered with a simple "yes." That was it. No need for the statistics I had prepared or the positive outcomes of international experiences I had researched. I asked, he approved, and off to Greece I went.

About three weeks into the semester, two of my classmates and I decided to take a weekend trip to Santorini. As the trip came to a close and we waited to board the plane back to Thessaloniki, the girls and I sat in the airport and spoke about our families. As I listened to them recount family vacations, verbal displays of affection, and all the things that get crammed into a Hallmark film, I felt a twinge of jealousy—that wasn't how my family operated at all. The storybook dinner table conversations about how our days went and the joyful "Good job, Champ" after sports competitions were not commonplace in my home. Instead, my home was a constant roller coaster of love, frustration, fear, and sadness, and as I listened to them, my jealously morphed into what I can now only describe as contentment and acceptance.

Growing up, my family was never into mushy, gushy expressions of love, but love was there. It was expressed in daily readings from the This Day in History section of our local newspaper. While I don't remember half of what I read, I have no doubt that the ritual is going to help me win *Jeopardy!* one day. And speaking of that show, that was another expression of love. My siblings and I watched it and *Wheel of*

*Fortune*[15] each weeknight, right before reading a passage out of the book of Psalms,[16] and going to bed at eight o'clock.[17]

I thought about those memories on the flight all the way back to Thessaloniki, and when I arrived at my apartment close to midnight, I logged on to Skype and called my dad's cell phone. I hadn't spoken to anyone back home since the previous weekend and couldn't wait to share all that I had seen with them. The phone rang and it connected, but instead of hearing my dad's heavy accent on the other line, it was my mom who answered. This immediately struck me as weird because she never really answered his phone. For a brief, naïve moment, I wondered if this meant that they were in a good place—maybe I had called while they were sitting together in the living room, watching one of those singing competitions they were so fond of.

The illusion quickly evaporated as my mom asked why I had called my dad's cell phone, and my naïvety was quickly replaced with frustration.

"Can't I go down the line?" I asked.

This I distinctly remember asking. I always called my dad

---

**15** Sometimes, if we could agree on another option, my brother, sister, and I would sneakily switch between these and other shows. #rebels #whogon'checkus #wequicklychangedbackwhentheparentsshowedup

**16** This practice in and of itself was a little odd considering that I stopped going to Sunday school when I was around seven or eight and my family stopped going to church around the same time. However, I guess the spirit of the written Word can stand on its own outside the brick-and-mortar factories where it is dissected and (mis)interpreted.

**17** I was a grandma before claiming to be a grandma was hip.

first in order to maintain a balance, and she knew this. They hardly ever used the landline in our house, so I called his cell phone,[18] spoke with him, then he passed the phone to her, we spoke, and then she passed it on to my little sister.[19]

The moments after this, however, are a blur, and today I struggle to relive them as they occurred rather than how I remember them.[20] I remember her pause, and then her soft voice coming through my headphones. This I know is probably true because my mother has a voice that wraps around you like cashmere, and due to the time difference, I would have been sitting on the outside balcony so I wouldn't wake up my roommate. I remember hearing her say something about how we knew this would happen. Something about them trying to reach me but not knowing how. I remember hearing her words and knowing she was trying to tell me something, but whatever it was wasn't registering. It was as foreign as the language I had been immersed in for the last few weeks.

I asked her to put my father on the phone because I needed to talk to him and then... nothing. There is a permanent gap in my memory at this point that picks back up with my roommate standing at the door, a concerned look on her face.

---

**18** My dad was one of those old people who kept his phone on a belt clip so that it was always within reach.

**19** My older brother was out of college and out of the house by this point.

**20** Memory is such an interesting concept. How much of our life actually occurred as it did in that moment versus how we have reimagined it in our memory? This reimagination can be accidental or, if we are too afraid to face what is as it was, intentional as we rearrange and repackage our lived experiences into something that is more digestible.

Using the process of elimination, I'm guessing this missing piece is the point when my mother told me the news—earlier that week my father had passed away in his sleep.

There were times throughout my life where I wondered how I would react when my father passed away. While he was, as he often proudly stated, as strong as a lion,[21] he was also the same age as some of my peers' grandparents, so I was keenly aware of his mortality. When thinking of his passing, I always envisioned what Life A.V. (After Von) would be like. I envisioned freedoms and laughter. I envisioned family trips that wouldn't get canceled on the planned date of departure and money that wouldn't be "borrowed" for "car repairs" (read: lottery tickets). Even as I envisioned what the aftermath of his passing would look like, I never really thought about the moment itself, the moment when the loss would occur or when the absence would register. I now know that nothing in my wildest imagination would compare to the real thing, because when my mother told me that my father had died while I was thousands of miles away, all I could do was scream. I wanted to speak with him, and I was being told that I couldn't. None of it made sense.

In the days that followed, I found myself embarrassed by this reaction. I had woken up my roommate, a girl I had known for less than a month, and had to explain what had happened. I had to deal with random bursts of tears in the

---

21 This comparison was true—I don't think I ever saw him sick while I was growing up.

middle of class surrounded by people who could do nothing for me. And the weeks that followed were no better. Every time I would do something amazing, I would be transported back to the reality of what waited for me in the states. Every time I went to explore different opportunities with my classmates, I was gripped with the fear of what was happening back home while I was enjoying myself. I felt guilty for continuing on as though nothing in my life had changed while my family was surrounded by constant reminders of what we had lost, and every time I thought I had a handle on it, something would pop up to show me how wrong I was.

On one occasion, I was in Athens for a school-sponsored trip, and some of my classmates and I went into an art gallery before dinner. As everyone looked around and spoke with the artist/owner, I came across a painting of a solitary man sitting on a chair, his back rounded with age, and the sepia lines on his face holding a lifetime of stories. The tears came before I could stop them, and I walked outside to collect myself before anyone could see. When I went back inside, I bought a different painting from the artist, and it currently hangs in my mother's dining room. As I stood in the gallery, I didn't think I would be able to handle having the painting of the man in my possession, not if it was going to cause that type of reaction. Today, leaving it behind is one of my biggest regrets.

In the end, after discussing my plans with my mom, I decided to finish the semester in Greece. Returning home would have served no purpose—all I could do there was sit and cry and/or console other people who were crying—and education was always at the top of my dad's priority list. Finishing the semester was the only thing I could do to be of value. In my heart I knew that continuing the journey he'd sent me on would make him proud.

When the semester ended and I arrived back home, I hovered at the front door for a few shaky breaths before walking in, unsure of what would be on the other side. When I was in Greece, I was surrounded with a new language and a new way of life—that confusion was expected. Now that I was home, I felt more lost than ever before. Not only was my father not there to greet me and hear about my adventures, but it also seemed as though my family had fully adjusted to Life A.V. They had grieved together and said as much of a goodbye as they could, and there I was, a visitor who arrived tardy to the sadness party and who would soon be leaving to live my life back at school.

To this day, I haven't visited my father's grave. I don't think I'm quite ready to—as it stands, it took me years to ask what caused his death.[22] Looking back, perhaps I am still not quite ready to fully accept that he is gone, not because I didn't know that it could happen, but because I'm still coming to terms with the way it did. This lack of acceptance has taken

---

22 Emotionally I know I'm deflecting, but this is something that I actually need to be better at because, from my understanding, it was an undiagnosed heart condition. As I consider my future health and that of any children I may have, these are important things to be aware of. So reader, even though I haven't quite done so myself yet, you should really try to learn your family's medical history.

several forms throughout the years, some more benign than others. In the safest, simplest form, I wear his ring as my own, a symbol of who he was and the role he played in my life. In the minutes, days, and weeks immediately after learning the news of his death, this shock and denial took the form of risky behaviors such as taking late-night walks alone in a foreign country to clear my head and consuming heavy amounts of alcohol.

In *Fences* by August Wilson, the main character's mantra is that he's doing the best he can,[23] and isn't that usually the case? Aren't we all trying to do the best we can with what we have at any given moment? I now know that, for better and for worse, everything I am and everything I will be is based on my life D.V. (During Von). While there are elements of my upbringing that I wouldn't wish on anyone, there is so much that I wish everyone had an opportunity to experience. We may not have been a Hallmark movie, but I know that I was blessed with someone who would have moved heaven and earth if he needed to. He did the best he could and that was enough.

---

23 *Fences* was written by August Wilson in 1985 and follows Troy Maxson, a man whose unfulfilled dreams take center stage in his relationship with his wife, Rose; their son, Cory; and other individuals in his life. Originally crafted as a play, Wilson's work was brought to the big screen by Denzel Washington and Viola Davis in 2016, and chills ran down my spine as I watched. So much of the film resonated with me, and it brought a closure I didn't know I needed. I highly suggest you watch it at some point.

CHAPTER 7: An Immigrant's Tale

MY FATHER CAME TO AMERICA from Jamaica in 1984 and—as legend has it—originally planned to stay in the United States only for a few months. However, he ended up putting down roots in Mount Vernon, New York, and remained in the states until he passed away in 2009. My mother joined him in 1987, and I was added to the mix in 1989, making me a first-generation American.

As I get older and navigate the ups and downs of life, I'm constantly rendered speechless when I think about the sacrifices my parents made. My father came to the United

States to help my grandmother; he knew nothing about this new land and had to start his life all over. He used to share stories of those first few months in the states, and there are a couple I always remember when I'm confronted with moments of confusion and uncertainty.

In one story, he was preparing to run errands one February afternoon, and after seeing the sun shining brightly outside, he walked out without a jacket. While there was no snow on the ground and none on the horizon, he received a rude awakening when the frigid cold smacked him in the face. If anyone has experienced a February day in New York, you know firsthand that the sun is a liar and has nothing to do with the blistering cold temperatures outside. In that moment, he learned how difficult something as seemingly simple as weather could be to navigate.

In another, he applied for a job, got the offer, and went in for his first day, only to be told when he arrived that the position was actually filled by someone else. When he recounted the incident to someone, they let him in on a secret—he wasn't the first person that had happened to, and he wouldn't be the last. The employer was known to not hire black people, and the only reason why my dad made it as far in the process as he did was because of his white-sounding name. For the remainder of his time in the United States, my father encountered moments where the identity he carried his whole life became a stumbling block to his aspirations and goals. For a man who was a successful businessman in Jamaica, having to go through these rudimentary, bleak lessons must have been a painful, humbling experience.

Like millions of other immigrants, my parents constantly chose between A and B so that my siblings and I could have the rest of the alphabet available to us. They chose to navigate uncertainty and challenges so that we could have the opportunity to live life as we wanted. They stared at closed doors so that we could decline things by choice and not miss out by lack of chance. With that bravery, resilience, and hope running through my veins, how dare I be scared of any challenge that comes my way? How dare I shrink myself to fit into the molds that others put in front of me? How dare I be less than great?

The answer is I don't—I don't dare squander this gift. Onward and upward. To infinity and beyond.[24]

---

**24** Shout-out to *Toy Story*, a film series with possibly the best finale ever.

INT. ISABELLA STEWART GARDNER MUSEUM — DAY

Inside the long hall of a gallery at late
afternoon, the sun is casting long shadows
against walls of oil paintings. Bethany
and Olivia walk casually through, stopping
periodically to view paintings and statues.

                    OLIVIA
          So, this law firm. Do you like it?


                    BETHANY
          I do. Not gonna lie, I got into it
          mostly because of my parents and the
          money, but I like what I'm doing.

Olivia makes a noncommittal sound and walks
away.


                    BETHANY
          Thoughts? Sounds like you have a
          comment about that.

Olivia shrugs, her eyes trained on a statue leaning against the wall.

                    OLIVIA
          Nothing in particular, just taking in
          what you said.

Bethany faces Olivia directly, arms crossed and her weight resting on one hip.

                    OLIVIA
          What happened to your interest in
          social work? I remember you wanting
          to go into MSW programs after
          graduation.

                    BETHANY
          I did. I applied to some, but also
          applied to law schools, and when I
          got into a program that let me do
          both, I went for it.

She turns back to look at the wall, her eyes focusing on a different piece.

                    BETHANY
          I started the pro bono program at my
          firm that partners with local women's
          and family shelters.

Olivia turns to look at her.

                    BETHANY
          Surprised?

She moves down the line to take in the next
piece.

                    BETHANY
          You shouldn't be. And you shouldn't
          be so judgy either.

                    OLIVIA
               (chastised)
          Sorry.

                    BETHANY
          There's nothing wrong with money, you
          know, or with not wanting to not be
          broke. The only time it becomes wrong
          is if you intentionally hurt other
          people to make it.

The two walk into the next room.

                    BETHANY
          How about you? You started to talk
          about this MBA program and how you
          decided against it.

                    OLIVIA
              (her voice noncommittal)
          It just wasn't for me.


                    BETHANY
          What about it wasn't for you?


                    OLIVIA
              (narrowing her eyes)
          Are you going to psychoanalyze me?


Bethany holds up her hands in surrender.


                    OLIVIA
          Because I already have a therapist,
          thank you very much. You take one
          psychology class and all of a sudden
          you're the all-knowing intuitive
          mind.


She rolls her eyes.


                    OLIVIA
          But yeah, I took some classes and
          didn't like the vibe of the program
          as I got more into it. It may be the
          program itself, but...


She shrugs.

                         OLIVIA
          I haven't given much thought to
          trying a different school, but I
          haven't necessarily ruled it out,
          either.


                         BETHANY
          What are you doing with the start-up
          you mentioned?


                         OLIVIA
          I'm basically making sure they're
          considering real people in what
          they're doing. It's a health app that
          connects folks with doctors based
          on specialty, demographics, medical
          history, ratings...stuff like that.


The women walk to another section of the museum.


                         OLIVIA
          I like them a lot, and I think they
          can do a lot of good work. It's just
          a matter of making sure they're
          keeping all communities in mind as
          they provide recommendations.


                         BETHANY
          Do you think you'll stick with them
          for a long time?

                    OLIVIA
          At this point, yes. Each day is
          different, so I'm not bored, which is
          important. I also buy into the work
          we're doing, which is crucial.

They stop to look closer at different pieces and
read the attached descriptions.

                    OLIVIA
          Do you see yourself staying at the
          firm for a long time?

                    BETHANY
          Uh...yeah.

She pauses before continuing.

                    BETHANY
          I mean...I enjoy the work, and I
          like that I'm able to do the pro bono
          stuff.

Olivia gives her a pointed look.

                    OLIVIA
          But...

Bethany returns Olivia's look before shifting her attention to the wall.

                    BETHANY
          (sighing)
     But I feel like there's more I should
     be doing.

                    OLIVIA
     Like what?

                    BETHANY
     If I had it my way, I'd work directly
     with a shelter or nonprofit org.
     The corporate world is so full of
     it. People don't really care about
     the cases they're working on, and
     companies probably did what they're
     being accused of doing.

                    OLIVIA
          (raising an eyebrow)
     So basically you're saying that you
     love your job and you're finding value
     and a sense of self every time you
     walk through the door.

Bethany groans.

                    BETHANY
          Don't get me wrong, not everyone is
          like that, but enough of them are
          that it's gotten to the point where
          I don't know what the hell I'm doing
          there. I don't know if it's always
          been like that and I'm just now
          noticing it or if this is something
          new, but either way it sucks.

The two women walk toward a balcony overlooking
the courtyard.

                    OLIVIA
          So quit.

                    BETHANY
          And do what?

                    OLIVIA
          You just said you want to work more
          in the community, so...

                    BETHANY
          Yeah, but it's not that easy.

                    OLIVIA
          Why not? If you left and started
          doing something you actually found
          meaningful, what's the worst that

                    OLIVIA (CONT'D)
would happen?

                    BETHANY
Well, for one thing, there's really
no organization that does what I want
to do, so...

                    OLIVIA
Excuse number one. What else?

                    BETHANY
          (glaring at her)
So, I wouldn't be able to transition
into anything immediately. Plus, I'm
in the middle of cases and can't just
up and leave.

                    OLIVIA
          (holding up two fingers)
Excuse number two. Go on.

Bethany lets out a frustrated sigh.

                    OLIVIA
Have you spoken with Frederick about
it?

                    BETHANY
            (walking over to another piece)
        I've mentioned it in passing once
        or twice but haven't really said
        anything about it.

                    OLIVIA
        Why?

                    BETHANY
            (rolling her eyes)
        Because he would have pushed just
        like you are right now. I should have
        known better than to bring this up
        with you.


Olivia walks over to where Bethany is standing
and turns to look at the piece, too.

                    OLIVIA .
        It sounds like this is something you
        really want, but you're making up
        shitty excuses cuz you're scared to
        do it.

                    BETHANY
        They're not excuses, they're actual
        issues.

                         OLIVIA
              If you say so.


                         BETHANY
              They are!


                         OLIVIA
              I know you think that, so okay.


She pauses before continuing.


                         OLIVIA
              I'm just wondering when you'll stop
              letting them be issues that keep you
              from doing what you actually want
              instead of doing what's easy.

## CHAPTER 8: The Leftovers

WHAT IF THE GOOD THINGS that come to those who wait are just the leftovers from the eager beavers who got there first?

CHAPTER 9: Patience and Self-Assurance 101—
A Master Class with James Cameron

"If you set your goals ridiculously high and it's a failure,
you will fail above everyone else's success."

—James Cameron

WHEN *AVATAR* HIT THEATERS in 2009, it was the
first feature film that James Cameron wrote, produced, and
directed since *Titanic*. Released twelve years after the block-
buster that made Leonardo DiCaprio and Kate Winslet
household names, *Avatar* was surrounded by unmistakable
hype and fanfare. Between who Cameron was as a person[25] and what he set out to do, there were as many skep-
tics as there were supporters, but he moved forward anyway.

25 Cameron was known around Hollywood for high expectations and expensive
budgets, and some of his harshest critics said that he couldn't back any of it up.
If Instagram and Twitter were around back then, he probably would have posted
videos about his haters being his biggest motivators, with money raining down in the
background or something.

When the movie was finally completed, it had an estimated $237,000,000 price tag.[26] During its opening weekend, it played on over three thousand screens across the country and brought in $77,025,481. Nineteen days after its premiere, *Avatar* surpassed the $1 billion threshold internationally, and by November 2010, the film had earned $760,507,625 in the United States alone. Despite its lukewarm reception from movie critics, Cameron's project was a commercial success.

I saw the film in theaters and went for the 3-D experience, which meant I had to wear two pairs of glasses at once. From what I can remember, the movie was cute. Very much a white savior narrative and reminiscent of Disney's *Pocahontas*, but cute nonetheless. As much as the story line was a common trope, we're not gonna talk about that right now. Instead, what I want to focus on is the fact that James Cameron started writing *Avatar* in 1994—over a decade before he released it for public consumption. While he had the idea of the film for years, he didn't act on it because the world wasn't big enough to give him what he needed. Cameron, for all his alleged ego and expectations, was fine waiting until he was able to do what he wanted in the exact way it deserved to be done.

Let that sink in a bit.

Rather than put something out just to say he did it, Cameron sat on the idea—one that I'm sure many people

---

26 Thank you, *Avatar*'s IMDB page, for these data points.

shook their heads at—and kept watch. There was no guarantee that the technology would ever become available, much less that he would have access to the tools if and when they did, and yet he still waited. And as technology and the movie industry slowly caught up to him, he took it upon himself to put the exact pieces he needed in place. He developed a language.[27] He made sure those taking part in his vision knew exactly what he wanted to bring to life.[28] And through it all, he waited.

I provide that background to ask this: What is your *Avatar?* What is your idea that you absolutely know will be a game changer, the thing that keeps you up burning the midnight oil?

At this very moment, are you able to bring it to life in the exact way you've envisioned it? If so, are you? If not, are you willing to wait?

I don't know what my *Avatar* is yet—maybe it's this book, maybe it's getting my doctorate before I'm thirty-five—but I do know this: We owe it to ourselves not to cut corners. We owe it to our dreams and our passions to remain true and steadfast in the belief that they are worthy of being nurtured until they can reach their final form.

---

27 According to Ed Power's article "Avatar: How the Biggest Film of All Time Got Left Behind," published on April 15, 2016, in the *Telegraph*, Cameron worked with a linguist to create the 1,000-word Na'vi language that drew inspiration from Ethiopian and Maori dialects.

28 In preparation for her role, one of the stars of the film, Sigourney Weaver, was required to study with a professor of plant physiology so she could fully understand Cameron's vision for the way her character would connect with vegetative life.

This can apply to our professional lives, to our personal lives, and essentially to anything to which we dedicate our time and our energy.

Are you willing to wait?

Are you willing to put faith in the unknown simply on the belief of what could be?

Are you willing to make the most of the thread laid out for you, even though you have no idea how long your piece is?

Now I'm going to take a moment to make an important distinction here: Waiting for the perfect opportunity is not the same as being immobile and inactive. It is not the same as being paralyzed by fear of inadequacy or by the need for perfection. I know firsthand the pain of that wait. It's what made sitting down and taking this idea out of my mind and putting it onto a computer screen for you to read so hard.[29]

When I talk about waiting for the perfect opportunity, I'm talking about seizing the moment in which you have no other choice but to act—when all of your work and the signs you've been waiting for come together like your personal North Star and point in the same direction.

From the time he came up with the concept in 1994 to when the film was released in 2009, Cameron worked on numerous projects, including nineteen feature films, over

---

29 Jenni Barrett writes so wonderfully about this in her piece "You Aren't Lazy— You're Just Terrified: On Paralysis and Perfectionism," https://ravishly.com/you-ar-ent-lazy-youre-just-terrified-paralysis-and-perfectionism-mental-health. Truth be told, I had to read that article a couple of times as I put this project together.

one hundred episodes of TV programming, and seven video games.[30] He lived his life. He continued creating, learning, growing, and gathering the skills and resources he needed to make his goal more attainable.

Can you imagine what must have been going through his mind all those years? To see other films being made during that time? Cameron's world is one where products are constantly developed and released, where success can be slow to achieve and quick to disappear, and where consumer interest ebbs and flows, but still he waited because he knew that what he envisioned was so much greater than what was available to him.

And this is the challenge I have for myself and the challenge I share with you. In the midst of so much change and a seemingly never-ending loop of successes and triumphs that you watch from the sidelines, will you wait? Will you have faith in the process and faith in your goals? Will you trust in your ability to move beyond the limitations and barriers you create for yourself and channel your energy in ways that you never have before?

In whatever it is that you're doing, whatever it is that's keeping you up at night, as Cameron says in his 2010 TED talk, failure is an option, but fear isn't. You will fail, most likely several times. These moments when you fall down are an unavoidable fact of life, but there's nothing that says you

---

30  Again, thank you, IMDB.

have to be afraid on the way down, especially not if that fear is of yourself and who you could be if you got out of your own way.[31]

Even as you're waiting for your dream production, you don't stop working. You keep making little projects and taking little steps to build up your capital, to learn the lay of the land, and to get people to trust in what you can bring to the table. Even when it seems like your peers are moving light-years ahead of you, just wait. Have faith in yourself and in the way things are lining up. There is no timeline for success, no benchmark by which you should be measuring your progress. The notion that we have to have certain things accomplished by a certain time needs to change, and while you can't control what the outside world focuses on, you can control where you put your attention and how you measure your own progress. After all, your own blue aliens are waiting on the other side.

---

[31] One of my dear friends once said to me that her version of hell would be, at the end of her life, meeting the person she could have been if she had just pushed past every fear or excuse that tried to get in her way. I think about that so often. Obviously, having a healthy dose of fear in life is necessary—it keeps us alive and helps ensure rational decision-making—but some fears are just an enemy of progress. I'm currently working on having the wisdom to tell which is which, and I imagine it will be an ongoing project.

# CHAPTER 10: Burning the Midnight Oil

IN "SIDELINE STORY,"[32] JERMAINE COLE (professionally known as J. Cole) invites us into what he imagines to be the mind of Coretta Scott before she added "King" to her name and before Martin became the beloved[33] icon he is

---

**32** I can't reprint the lyrics because of copyright laws, but I really suggest you go look them up yourself and/or listen to the track.

**33** Martin Luther King, Jr. has become such a fascinating case study on the ways someone's life can be commandeered, sterilized, reimagined, and reframed. His name and ethos is usually invoked to chastise people who call out injustices in "disruptive" ways, and each year, like clockwork, select excerpts from the catalogue of his life's work are highlighted. However, few textbooks share the footnote that he spent nearly a third of his life being monitored by the FBI who described him as "the most dangerous and effective Negro leader in the country" after he gave that often quoted speech.

today. He spends a portion of the first verse musing about whether or not Scott had any idea about the dreams King had, or the hopes he carried for himself and those around him. Cole embeds his wondering in reflections of his own journey, and for me, these bars perfectly capture the secrets and fears we might carry when we're not quite sure if we're ready for the success we painstakingly long for.[34] Whenever I'm looking for motivation, I usually follow this track with "Blessings" by Chancelor Bennett (Chance the Rapper) who asks if we're ready for our miracle. As I look back at where I've been and ahead to where I'm going, I can honestly say that I'm trying to be, each and every day.

I know that I'm a talented person, but there's still a little voice in the back of my head that whispers, "But what if you *aren't* as amazing as you think you are?" This voice is sly and seductive, and sometimes it can be very persuasive.[35] It's stopped me from raising my hand in classrooms. It's guided my mouse away from job applications. It's kept me from picking up the phone to see if people want to hang out. It almost kept this chapter out of a book that it almost kept from being published.

While I may know in my heart of hearts that I haven't reached my final form yet, there's still the fear that one day I'll discover that where I am is as far as I'll go and—sacré

34 I know that the verse goes on to discuss King's alleged infidelity, but just walk with me along this path, okay?

35 To be honest, if I had to give a voice to it, it would sound just like Kaa (the snake) in the 1967 cartoon version of *The Jungle Book*.

bleu!—I've peaked. Or worse yet, I'll discover that where I am is a fluke, and I can't recreate or build on it if I tried.[36]

I'm not a religious person by any means. The last time I set foot in a church was for a couple of weddings in the summer of 2016, and the time before that was probably in high school. However, while I'm not really committed to the Holy Word as it's been crafted and defined by my fellow humans, I do believe in a higher power that goes far beyond my comprehension.[37] Because of this, I fully believe that the Big (Wo) Man Upstairs[38] doesn't give anyone more than they can handle. With this Truth guiding my steps, lately I've been hitting the prayer gym so I can build some Holy Muscle because, as Bennett excitedly says, when the praises go up, the blessings come down.

For me, this means speaking what I want into existence, because if I don't give voice to it, I'll never know how sweet it sounds. It means doing the things that terrify me the most, because this fear lets me know that I have something to lose if it goes wrong, but so much more to gain if it goes right. It means keeping my trusted supporters close and letting them

---

**36** Imposter Syndrome is real, y'all.

**37** This belief was solidified by the solar eclipse on August 21, 2017. My goodness. As I watched the moon pass over the sky during totality and heard the crickets come to life as "night" fell in the middle of the day, I had no doubt that there's a master artist at work. It was such a beautiful, humbling, spiritual experience, and I currently have a photo NASA took of the moment as the background on my phone, just so I can remember that sliver of peace throughout all the chaos of life.

**38** How I refer to the entity that is supposedly the all-knowing, all-seeing Creator.

hold up a mirror so I can see what gets reflected back, because sometimes my vision is so cloudy that I can't see what's in front of me. It means channeling my inner Kanye Pope[39] and standing in my greatness, because if I don't, no one else can or will.

At the end of the day, we're all on the brink of greatness. Some of us have plans that no one but us and a god know about. Some of us haven't even dared to speak them out loud for fear of what the echo would sound like. But we can only hope and trust that the dreams being dreamed, the schemes being schemed, and the work we do in the dark will be enough to get (or keep) us off the sidelines. As someone[40] once said, you have to stay ready so you don't have to get ready. So, are you?

---

39 Kanye Pope is who I imagine Kanye West would be if he had Olivia Pope serving as his speechwriter or translator. This individual has the confidence of Kanye with the poise and finesse of Olivia. Truly a winning combo.

40 Not sure who you are, Mystery Originator, but this is such a schnazzy motto. Thanks!

INT. ISABELLA STEWART GARDNER MUSEUM — DAY (LATER)

Bethany and Olivia continue to walk and browse.

> BETHANY
> I just wish there was a noticeable
> sign of some sort when the one for
> you is in your vicinity. An alarm. Or
> a horn. Something.

> OLIVIA
> Could you imagine, though? All those
> bells and whistles going off all day,
> every day, and never knowing who
> prompted it or if it's even for you?

> BETHANY
> Maybe it's only heard by the
> person it's for. Like I get my own
> notification and no one else does
> since it's not for them.

                    OLIVIA
        But what happens if the person who
        triggers your notification doesn't
        get one in return? Like, would you
        be able to know if it was a mutual
        "ding," or would you just be all
        awkward like "OMG did you hear that?"
        and the person's all like "Nah"?


                    BETHANY
        Oh...that would suck.


                    OLIVIA
        Right? Or imagine if you're all the
        way through what you consider to be a
        fulfilling life—married with children
        and grandchildren and a great job,
        you know, the works—and you're out
        grocery shopping or something and
        hear an alarm. A horn. Something.
        Does that mean your life wasn't full
        of love and happiness before that
        moment? Is there only one alarm, or
        are there multiple moments of "The
        One"?


She pauses for a beat.


                    OLIVIA
        Does it vary by the type of love?

                    OLIVIA (CONT'D)
          What if you wander the world trying
          to hear a bell and find out at the
          end that you ignored the many
          opportunities for happiness that were
          in front of you along the way? That
          you essentially missed out on the
          joys of the "here and now" in search
          of a future that didn't exist?

                       BETHANY
               (sighing)
          Okay, so maybe it wouldn't work.

                       OLIVIA
          No, this isn't me saying that it
          couldn't work. I'm just saying I
          don't think we need a whole new set
          of notifications for things we already
          do every single day of our lives.

EXT. ISABELLA STEWART GARDNER MUSEUM - DAY

The women walk out of the museum and rejoin the
city outside its walls. In silence they turn
left and begin down the block, retracing their
steps back to where they started. As they walk,
Bethany turns to look at Olivia.

                    BETHANY
What do you mean?

                    OLIVIA
I mean, we already walk around
oblivious to things that are sometimes
right in front of us. Why do we need
special notifications when we already
have ways of letting people know how
we feel? We can call, we can text,
we can write, hell, we can even send
carrier pigeons...If we ignore all
of these, who's to say that we'll
suddenly start paying attention to
some other type of notification?

                    BETHANY
          (nodding slowly)
True.

                    OLIVIA
I mean, what was your notification?

                    BETHANY
My notification?

                    OLIVIA
With Frederick. What was your
notification?

                    BETHANY
          (smiles)
I don't know the exact moment per
se. I just know one minute we were
catching up after some time apart
and the next I'm looking at him and
realizing that he was exactly who
I had been searching for this whole
time.


                    OLIVIA
See, and you didn't even need an
alarm to tell you that.


                    BETHANY
What about you?


                    OLIVIA
What about me?


                    BETHANY
Have you gotten a notification?


                    OLIVIA
I've dated some guys here and there,
but none of the people I've met
have been worth investing the time
and energy needed for a successful
relationship.

She shrugs.

                    OLIVIA
          Have I met guys that, in hindsight,
          could have prompted a notification?
          Absolutely. But since I usually go
          into things with the expectation of
          something temporary, I don't really
          allow myself to imagine or look for
          things that would signal something
          permanent.

                    BETHANY
               (nodding)
          Is that something you'd like to
          change?

                    OLIVIA
               (tilting her head as she thinks)
          Um...I guess so. I mean, my focus
          has always been on other aspects of
          my life, but now I have the time to
          look at the personal side, so I guess
          that's a start.

                    BETHANY
          I feel like there's something that
          you're not saying.

                    OLIVIA
          Like what?

                    BETHANY
          I don't know, but I do know that
          you're not one to shy away from
          things, so why start now?

Olivia rolls her eyes.

                    OLIVIA
          It's nothing, really. Just talking
          with you about this makes me think
          of this guy I dated for a little in
          Portland.

                    BETHANY
          I knew it!

                    OLIVIA
          There's really nothing to know. We
          dated. He was great, but again, it's
          all about focus. At the time, I
          wasn't really interested in doing the
          whole "Oh, here's my entire feelings
          gallery. Feel free to wander around,
          but don't break anything" thing.

                    BETHANY
          And now?

                    OLIVIA
          And now what?

                    BETHANY
          How do you feel about it now?

Olivia lets out a frustrated sigh.

                    OLIVIA
          And now I can't help but wonder what
          would have happened had I approached
          things differently.

                    BETHANY
          Are you gonna call him?

                    OLIVIA
     Who?

                    BETHANY
     Portland!

                    OLIVIA
     Why?

                    BETHANY
     Why not?

                    OLIVIA
          I don't even have his number anymore.

                         BETHANY
          Excuse number one. What else?

Olivia tosses her a look. Bethany returns it.

                         OLIVIA
          Don't know if you've looked at a map
          recently, but Boston is nowhere close
          to Portland.

                         BETHANY
          Excuse number two. Any others?

                         OLIVIA
               (after a beat)
          Do you feel better now?

                         BETHANY
          What was it that you said earlier?

She tilts her head and taps her chin.

                         BETHANY
               (snapping her fingers)
          Ah yes. I'm just wondering when those
          will stop being issues that keep you
          from doing what you actually want
          instead of what's easy.

                    OLIVIA
              (rolling her eyes)
          Whatever.

The two continue walking, Olivia shaking her
head and Bethany's laugh trailing behind them.

## Chapter 11: I Can't Guarantee You'll Be Safe

"To go it alone or to go with a partner. When you choose a partner you have to have compromises and sacrifices, but it's the price you pay. Do I want to follow my every whim and desire as I make my way through time and space? Absolutely. But at the end of the day, do I need someone when I'm doubting myself and I'm insecure and my heart's failing me? Do I need someone who, when the heat gets hot, has my back?...I do."

—*Safety Not Guaranteed* [41]

THAT'S IT. HERE'S TO patiently building my time machine until the right partner comes along to take that leap of faith with me.[42]

---

[41] *Safety Not Guaranteed* is a 2012 comedy-drama (dramedy?) where Mark Duplass plays Kenneth, a supermarket clerk who believes he's figured out how to travel through time. Kenneth places an ad in the paper looking for travel buddies, and characters played by Aubrey Plaza, Jake Johnson, and Karan Soni respond to it. A heartwarming journey ensues. Great film. Go watch it.

[42] Even though, to be honest, I wouldn't want a time machine in real life because, as a black woman, I actually have no interest in traveling to the past. Unless I could go directly to a Michael Jackson or Sam Cooke concert or something and leave right after, no thank you—history shows that the past wasn't too kind to black people.

## CHAPTER 12: Things I Love
### (in No Particular Order)

LYRICS THAT MAKE MY HEART sing along. combinations of words and punctuation marks that speed up my heartbeat and take my breath away. love. peanut m&m's. crispy pad thai. sushi. Jamaican food. Greek chocolate. Oreo cheesecake. food in general. laughing so hard that my abdominal muscles ache. crème brûlée. hugs from people I want to hug. awkward situations. mentally adding "that's what she said" where (in)appropriate. smiling. kindness. art. reading. walking. running. driving fast. silence that speaks volumes. that look. people who deserve it. helping others.

finding myself. tall boots. when I find that one nail polish color that I'll never not use again. music. car chase scenes. psychological thrillers. mushy gushy crap. wit. sarcasm. cooking. rings. leather jackets. reciprocity. old-school songs. being random. going to concerts alone. midnight walks with no destination. anything that makes me feel the way the first person to hear the drum solo in Phil Collins' "In the Air Tonight" probably felt. libraries. museums. he who, as of now, remains unnamed, unknown, unseen, and undiscovered.

EXT. A STREET IN DOWNTOWN BOSTON — DAY

Bethany and Olivia are stopped in the middle of
the sidewalk, facing each other.

                    BETHANY
          Well...

                    OLIVIA
          Well.

                    BETHANY
          We should do this again.

                    OLIVIA
          We won't.

                    BETHANY
          Awfully pessimistic, aren't we.

                    OLIVIA
          I like to think of it as realistic.

                         BETHANY
          What makes you so certain?

                         OLIVIA
          Because you're gonna go back to your
          life and I'm gonna go back to mine.
          We've both been doing fine so far, so
          there's really no need to try and
          change things.

                         BETHANY
              (rolling her eyes)
          Why are you so negative?

                         OLIVIA
              (shrugging as she looks away)
          It is-

                         BETHANY
          -what it is. Yeah, I know.

          Olivia looks at her before speaking again.

                         OLIVIA
          Thanks for extending the invite. It
          really was good to see you.

                         BETHANY
          It was good to see you, too.

          She pauses.

                    BETHANY
          And I'm sorry.

                     OLIVIA
              (raising an eyebrow)
          Sorry for what?

                    BETHANY
          I don't know. For not being a better
          friend, I guess.

                     OLIVIA
              (waving her hand dismissively)
          That's nice that you wanna apologize,
          but you don't have to. Really. You're
          not a bad friend. You're just...

She lets out a heavy breath.

                     OLIVIA
          It's okay to not want or need to talk
          to people anymore, and I don't...

She pauses again, choosing her words carefully.

                     OLIVIA
          I know you hate not having everything
          wrapped up nicely with a bow, but we
          approach things differently and
          that's fine, too. I'm glad to know

                    OLIVIA (CONT'D)
          you and that's enough for me. So,
          don't apologize. If you're saying it
          because you genuinely want to, that's
          cool, I guess, but if you're doing it
          because you think I want or need to
          hear it, no thanks.

Bethany is silent before nodding.

                    BETHANY
          Well, okay then. It was good to see
          you.

                    OLIVIA
          Yup...Be well.

                    BETHANY
          You, too.

Bethany and Olivia look at each other one final
time before turning and walking in opposite
directions.

                    THE END

## CHAPTER 13: Bloodsuckers

CONTINUE TO MOVE THROUGH life like a raging river in hopes that you never become stagnant. Stagnant water is a breeding ground for mosquitos, and no one likes those bloodsuckers.

## CHAPTER 14: In Which Silence Is No Longer Deemed Golden

THIS IS FOR ALL THE PEOPLE who remain "silent" after screaming so loud that their throats are raw, their voices gone.

For those who have been vocal their entire lives but need a moment to rest.

For those whose voices echo through the void and bounce against a wall of people who claim to listen, hear, and understand but refuse to absorb what they're told.

For those who have seen this episode several times already and know that another opportunity to stand will come when this airs in syndication.

To the people who have finally found the strength and the words to speak—make your voice loud.

Perhaps you've been saving your energy and outrage for this very moment.

Saving your fear and indignation for what you consider to be a real reason to shout.

Waiting for something that hits a little closer to home.

We're glad you could join us—we've been waiting for you.

To those who remain "silent," know that I am with you.

With you as you walk into work and have to deal with being talked over, talked through, and talked about. Again.

With you as you go home and have to explain to those close to you why you're so damn tired. Again.

With you as you wonder how long these new voices will be this loud.

And to those who have been vocal in public but turn their back and oppress in private.

Who micro-aggress coworkers who look different than them.

Who ignore the support staff who make their jobs and lives easier.

To you I say, keep the rallying cries. Keep the signs.

They—and you—are meaningless in the grand scheme of things.

Silence will do.

# CHAPTER 15: After the Credits Roll

AND THIS, MY FRIENDS, is the end. The final chapter (of this book at least). True story, I wrote this chapter before the book was even completed. Even before I was sure I'd finish it. Wanna know why?

Because it's a trick.

It was a trick to get myself in the mind-set that the book will end, that there will be something to conclude, because at the time I didn't quite believe it.[43]

---

[43] See Chapter 9 for the mention of perfectionism procrastination and Chapter 10 for the mention about the Imposter Syndrome. I went back and forth about the way this project was set up and what I wanted to say so many times that I almost threw the whole thing away.

I don't really know that what I'm doing is worth it, that it will matter, and this, of course, is why it doesn't. Why it can't, at least not right now.

The weekend before I wrote this chapter, I was speaking with a friend about how George Orwell's *1984* saw nearly a 10,000 percent increase in sales[44] since 45[45] became president of the United States. As we spoke, I wondered out loud if Orwell had any idea how long his work would live on beyond him, and I have a feeling he didn't. I have a feeling that he just wrote because he had no other choice but to. Like Pablo Neruda muses about his love, I bet Orwell and those like him created things because they knew no other way.

That's the secret, isn't it? To work because you know no other way?

Similar to James Cameron and *Avatar*, you have to throw caution to the wind and wait until you can do justice to your dream. And not do justice in terms of success, but do justice so that when you sit back and think about what you've created, a sense of peace washes over you.

To work with the goal of success is a guaranteed failure if you define success by external metrics, because those will always change. People are fickle as hell and the marker will always move, especially when you get close to reaching it. But if you work with the goal of making yourself proud and

---

**44** Nope, this number isn't a typo or an exaggeration. Several outlets wrote about it in the days leading up to and after the innauguration.

**45** You know who I'm talking about, so I don't wanna hear it.

honoring your Truth, you can't go wrong because you get to define what those markers are. You get to define when you've made it. No one else.

So, there you have it.

My notes and observations. My questions and my thoughts.

A little piece of what I've been allotted. I hoped you enjoyed.

Ashe.

# Acknowledgments

TO MY PARENTS—there are no words (but I tried in a couple of chapters). Thank you.

To my committee: MR, TB, AB, SM, ST, SM, KYMM, and CH—your support through all stages of my life has been incomparable. Thanks for shooting with me in the gym and for always holding up a mirror.

To the creative minds behind my cover and internal layout: LM and MR—people *do* judge a book by its cover, and it *is* what's on the inside that counts. Thank you for taking my readers on a visual journey.

To my editing, bio development, and beta-reading team: JK, JZ, EL, CWR, KW, KHC, AC, and SG—your technical reviews, feedback, and questions helped this project reach its final form. Thank you.

To anyone not listed here explicitly—I forced myself to have a word count, but know that your thread helped make this tapestry what it is. Thank you.